DATE DUE

OCT 11 '99			
OCT 2 '01			

Venn, Cecilia.

That is not my hat

A Note to Parents

Welcome to REAL KIDS READERS, a series of phonics-based books for children who are beginning to read. In the classroom, educators use phonics to teach children how to sound out unfamiliar words, providing a firm foundation for reading skills. At home, you can use REAL KIDS READERS to reinforce and build on that foundation, because the books follow the same basic phonic guidelines that children learn in school.

Of course the best way to help your child become a good reader is to make the experience fun—and REAL KIDS READERS do that, too. With their realistic story lines and lively characters, the books engage children's imaginations. With their clean design and sparkling photographs, they provide picture clues that help new readers decipher the text. The combination is sure to entertain young children and make them truly want to read.

REAL KIDS READERS have been developed at three distinct levels to make it easy for children to read at their own pace.

- LEVEL 1 is for children who are just beginning to read.
- LEVEL 2 is for children who can read with help.
- LEVEL 3 is for children who can read on their own.

A controlled vocabulary provides the framework at each level. Repetition, rhyme, and humor help increase word skills. Because children can understand the words and follow the stories, they quickly develop confidence. They go back to each book again and again, increasing their proficiency and sense of accomplishment, until they're ready to move on to the next level. The result is a rich and rewarding experience that will help them develop a lifelong love of reading.

Produced by DWAI / Seventeenth Street Productions, Inc.

 Published by The Millbrook Press, Inc. Printed in the United States of America.

Library of Congress Cataloging-in-Publication Data

Venn, Cecilia.
That is not my hat / by Cecilia Venn ; photography by Dorothy Handelman.
p. cm. — (Real kids readers. Level 3)
Summary: When Kate's little brother loses his hat, Kate, Lisa, Max, and Nick all try to think of a plan to help him find it.
ISBN 0-7613-2008-3 (lib. bdg.). — ISBN 0-7613-2033-4 (pbk.)
[1. Lost and found possessions—Fiction. 2. Hats—Fiction.] I. Handelman, Dorothy, ill. II. Title. III. Series.
PZ7.V558Th 1998
[Fic]—dc21

97-31372
CIP
AC

pbk: 10 9 8 7 6 5 4 3 2 1
lib: 10 9 8 7 6 5 4 3 2 1

That Is *Not* My Hat!

Cecilia Venn

Photographs by Dorothy Handelman

The Millbrook Press
Brookfield, Connecticut

Kate, Lisa, Max, and Nick met at Pocket Park one fine morning. It was a good day to do something. But what?

Max dumped out his backpack. Stuff rolled everywhere. Nick drew a picture in his notebook. Lisa tried out a dance step.

"This is getting us nowhere," said Kate. "What can we do that's new?" She looked around the park, hoping for an idea.

Pocket Park was small, with houses on the sides and a gate at each end. But it was the perfect size for Kate and her friends. In fact, they met there almost every day.

"I've got it!" said Kate. "Let's start a club."

"What kind of club?" Nick asked.

"Will we have a clubhouse?" Lisa asked.

"Will there be snacks?" Max asked.

"We can think about all of that later," said Kate. "Just say yes if you want to be in a club."

"Yes," said Nick.

"Yes," said Lisa.

"Yes," said Max.

"Oh, oh, oh," moaned a voice behind Kate.

It was Kate's little brother, Sam. "Do you want to be in our club?" she asked him.

"Oh, oh, oh," Sam moaned again.

"I think Sam is trying to tell us something," Max said.

Everyone looked at Sam.

"My hat is gone," said Sam. "My best, best hat is gone."

Kate rolled her eyes. "What do you mean, gone? Where is your hat, Sam?"

“I was on my way here,” said Sam. “But all of a sudden, a big, strong wind hit me. It blew my hat right off my head! My hat flew over the house. It flew higher than the trees. That hat is going to the moon!”

Kate frowned. “It is not windy today, Sam. Where is your hat?”

Sam looked at his feet. “I don’t know,” he said sadly. “Will you guys help me find it?”

Everyone started talking at once.

"Wait!" cried Kate. "If we are going to find Sam's hat, we need a plan. Let's start looking here in Pocket Park. We can each pick a spot."

Lisa danced along the fence. She stood on a bench to peek over the railing.

Nick looked in the shed where the sports stuff was kept. He leaned over too far and fell into a box of balls.

Max dug in his pack and pulled out some string and a safety pin.

"What is that for?" asked Sam.

"This is my hat catcher," said Max. He tied the string to the open pin. "See? I toss out my line. Then, if your hat is there, I catch it." He started fishing in the tall grass.

Kate ran to the playground. She climbed to the top of the slide. She could see the whole park from there. But she could not see Sam's hat.

SLOANS

Kate slid down the slide. Nick met her at the bottom. "One thing is plain," Kate said. "This plan is not working."

Max joined them. "Did you say plane?" he said. "Look what I caught."

Kate and Nick laughed.

Sam started moaning again. “Oh, oh. This is bad! There is no sign of my hat anywhere.”

“Did you say sign?” Kate said. “That’s it! We’ll make a sign.”

“A Missing Hat sign,” said Lisa.

“It could be a Join Our Club sign too,” Kate said.

Nick went to get his markers. Sam and Lisa went to get some paper. Max tried to fly the plane.

The kids went to work. Soon they had five stacks of signs.

Max looked at Sam's stack. "You are missing something," he said.

"Yes," said Sam. "I am missing my hat."

"You are also missing an *s* in the word *missing,*" said Nick.

Sam fixed all his signs.

Kate wrote, "Join the Pocket Park Club" on her signs. "Okay," she said. "Let's go!"

"Wait," said Sam. "I need to get something first."

Sam ran home. When he came back, he was carrying a shoe box.

"What's that for?" asked Kate.

"I can't tell you. It's tap secret," said Sam.

"You mean, it's *top* secret," said Kate.

"No, I don't," said Sam. "Just wait. You'll see."

Kate rolled her eyes. "*Now* can we go?" she said.

"Sure," said Sam. "I'm ready."

Nick hung signs on the park gates. Max went with him. He taped a sign to the back of his airplane.

"What are you doing?" Nick asked.

"I'm making a flying sign," said Max. "I will send it all over town." He tossed the plane into the air, but it didn't go far.

"I don't know, Max," said Nick. "It's kind of hard to read upside down."

Missing Hats!
Bring found hats
to the park.
747 SPACE
SHUTTLE

Kate and Lisa went around the block. They stuck signs to trees. They left a sign at each house. They even taped one to Kate's own front door.

On their way back to Pocket Park, the girls saw a small crowd.

"Let's check it out," said Kate.

Lisa stood on her toes to see what was going on. "Hey! It's Sam!" she called to Kate.

"I lost my hat."

Tap, tap, tap.

"I want it back."

Tap, tap, tap.

Sam was tap dancing on the sidewalk. He handed out signs and sang loudly.

"I miss my hat."

Tap, tap, tap.

"I need it back."

Tap, tap, tap.

The girls clapped and cheered.

By noon all the signs were up.

"Let's eat!" said Max. "You can all come to my house for lunch."

The five kids set off. Sam was still dancing. *Tap, tap, tap.*

Later that day, they went back to the park.

"Oh, my!" said Lisa.

"Wow!" said Nick.

"Hats!" yelled Sam.

Hats spilled off the table. Hats hung on the gates. Hats were piled up on the grass.

Sam picked them up one by one. "This is not my hat. That is not my hat. Not my hat. Not my hat. Where is my hat?"

"Where are all the kids?" asked Kate. "Didn't anyone read the part about our club?"

Soon everyone was trying on hats.
“I like this one,” said Kate.
“That is not my hat,” said Sam.
“This one is cool,” Max said.
“That is not my hat,” said Sam.

“How do I look in this one?” asked Lisa.

“That is not my hat either,” said Sam.

“There are too many hats,” said Nick. “How will we ever find Sam’s?”

“We need a hat sorter,” said Max. “I will make one. Wait here.”

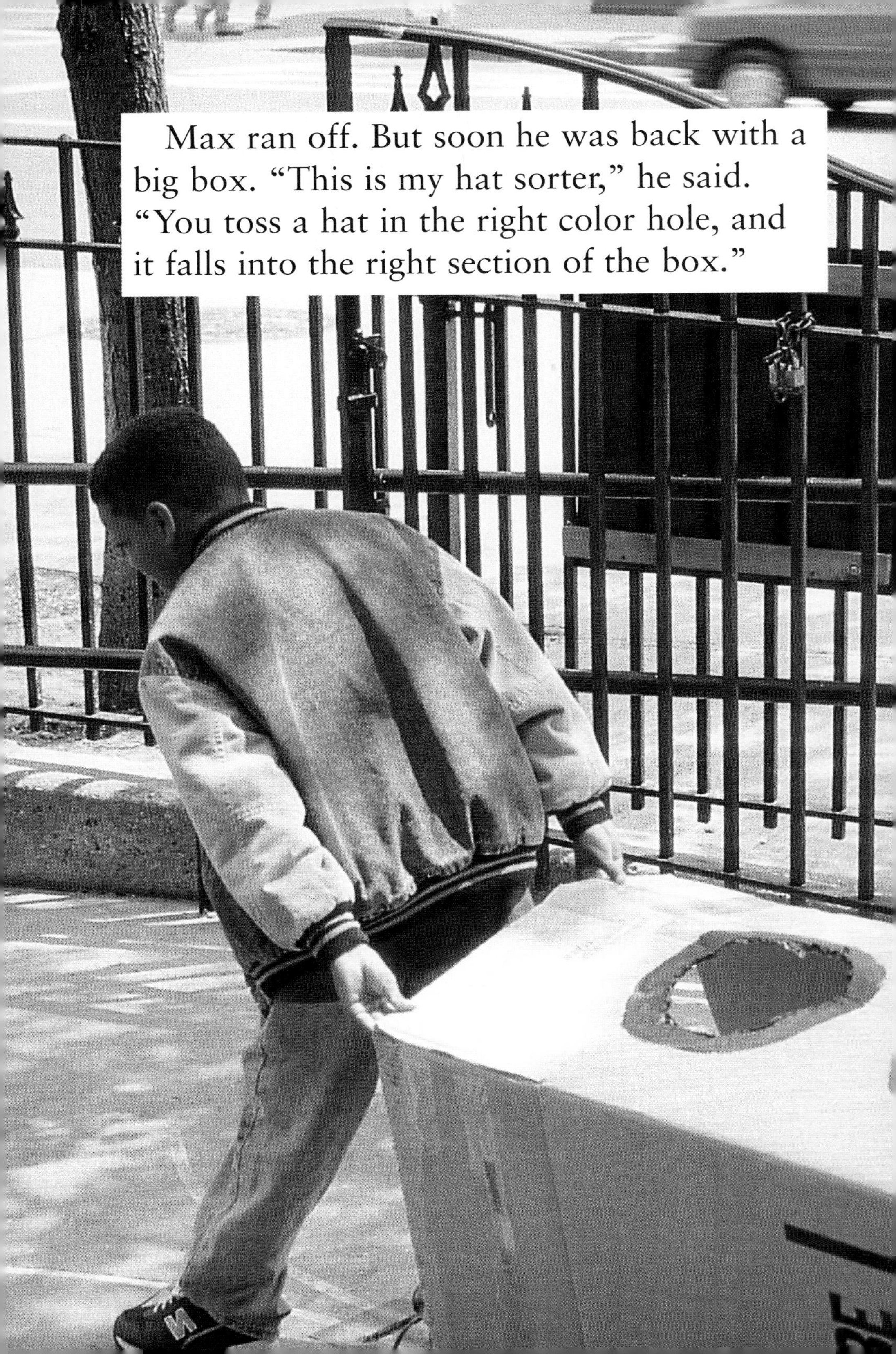

Max ran off. But soon he was back with a big box. "This is my hat sorter," he said. "You toss a hat in the right color hole, and it falls into the right section of the box."

"Cool," said Sam.

"Let's get sorting," said Lisa.

"I will watch the gate," said Kate. "Maybe someone will come to join our club."

The hat sorter was full in no time.

"What color is your hat?" Lisa asked Sam.

"Red," said Sam. He looked in the red hole of the hat sorter. There were lots of nice hats. But his hat was not there.

"What does your hat look like?" Nick asked. "I could draw a picture of it on each sign. Maybe that would help."

"Good idea!" said Kate. "Could you draw a clubhouse too?"

Nick just laughed.

Kate, Max, and Lisa gathered up all the signs. Sam told Nick what his hat looked like. Then Nick drew a big red hat on each sign. And Sam wrote his name under each hat.

The kids put up the signs again. They stopped for a quick snack. Then they went back to the park.

"Look! There's something on the hat sorter," yelled Sam.

"It's a note," said Lisa.

Kate picked it up and read it out loud. "I found your lost hat, but I can't bring it to Pocket Park. Go to the last yard on the left. Look up."

"Hey," said Sam. "That's *our* yard!"

The kids rushed to Sam and Kate's house. They looked around. No hat.

"The note said to look up," said Sam.

Five heads turned up.

"Yes!" yelled Sam. "*That* is my hat!"

"How did it get up there?" Kate asked.

Sam's face turned as red as his hat. "Well, I was climbing that tree two days ago," he said.

"Looks as if you'll be climbing it again very soon," said Max.

"That takes care of Sam's hat," said Lisa. "But what about all of the others?"

"Don't worry," said Kate. "I know just what to do with them."

The next day, there was a new sign on the gate to Pocket Park.

Join our club
meet at
the park
get a
free hat!

Reading with Your Child

Even though your child is reading more independently now, it is vital that you continue to take part in this important learning experience.

- Try to read with your child at least twenty minutes each day, as part of your regular routine.
- Encourage your child to keep favorite books in one convenient, cozy spot, so you don't waste valuable reading time looking for them.
- Read and familiarize yourself with the Phonic Guidelines on the next pages.
- Praise your young reader. Be the cheerleader, not the teacher. Your enthusiasm and encouragement are key ingredients in your child's success.

What to Do if Your Child Gets Stuck on a Word

- Wait a moment to see if he or she works it out alone.
- Help him or her decode the word phonetically. Say, "Try to sound it out."
- Encourage him or her to use picture clues. Say, "What does the picture show?"
- Encourage him or her to use context clues. Say, "What would make sense?"
- Ask him or her to try again. Say, "Read the sentence again and start the tricky word. Get your mouth ready to say it."
- If your child still doesn't "get" the word, tell him or her what it is. Don't wait for frustration to build.

What to Do if Your Child Makes a Mistake

- If the mistake makes sense, ignore it—unless it is part of a pattern of errors you wish to correct.
- If the mistake doesn't make sense, wait a moment to see if your child corrects it.
- If your child doesn't correct the mistake, ask him or her to try again, either by decoding the word or by using context or picture clues. Say, "Get your mouth ready" or "Make it sound right" or "Make it make sense."
- If your child still doesn't "get" the word, tell him or her what it is. Don't wait for frustration to build.

Phonic Guidelines

Use the following guidelines to help your child read the words in this story.

Short Vowels

When two consonants surround a vowel, the sound of the vowel is usually short. This means you pronounce *a* as in apple, *e* as in egg, *i* as in igloo, *o* as in octopus, and *u* as in umbrella. Words with short vowels include: *bed, big, box, cat, cup, dad, dog, get, hid, hop, hum, jam, kid, mad, met, mom, pen, ran, sad, sit, sun, top.*

R-Controlled Vowels

When a vowel is followed by the letter *r*, its sound is changed by the *r*. Words with *r*-controlled vowels include: *card, curl, dirt, farm, girl, herd, horn, jerk, torn, turn.*

Long Vowel and Silent E

If a word has a vowel followed by a consonant and an *e*, usually the vowel is long and the *e* is silent. Long vowels are pronounced the same way as their alphabet names. Words with a long vowel and silent *e* include: *bake, cute, dive, game, home, kite, mule, page, pole, ride, vote.*

Double Vowels

When two vowels are side by side, usually the first vowel is long and the second vowel is silent. Words with double vowels include: *boat, clean, gray, loaf, meet, neat, paint, pie, play, rain, sleep, tried.*

Diphthongs

Sometimes when two vowels (or a vowel and a consonant) are side by side, they combine to make a diphthong—a sound that is different from long or short vowel sounds. Diphthongs are: *au/aw, ew, oi/oy, ou/ow.* Words with diphthongs include: *auto, brown, claw, flew, found, join, toy.*

Double Consonants

When two identical consonants appear side by side, one of them is silent. Words with double consonants include: *bell, fuss, mess, mitt, puff, tall, yell.*

Consonant Blends

When two or more different consonants are side by side, they usually blend to make a combined sound. Words with consonant blends include: *bent, blob, bride, club, crib, drop, flip, frog, gift, glare, grip, help, jump, mask, most, pink, plane, ring, send, skate, sled, spin, steep, swim, trap, twin.*

Consonant Digraphs

Sometimes when two different consonants are side by side, they make a digraph that represents a single new sound. Consonant digraphs are: *ch, sh, th, wh*. Words with digraphs include: *bath, chest, lunch, sheet, think, whip, wish*.

Silent Consonants

Sometimes when two different consonants are side by side, one of them is silent. Words with silent consonants include: *back, dumb, knit, knot, lamb, sock, walk, wrap, wreck*.

Sight Words

Sight words are those words that a reader must learn to recognize immediately—by sight—instead of by sounding them out. They occur with high frequency in easy texts. Sight words include: *a, am, an, and, as, at, be, big, but, can, come, do, for, get, give, have, he, her, his, I, in, is, it, just, like, look, make, my, new, no, not, now, old, one, out, play, put, red, run, said, see, she, so, some, soon, that, the, then, there, they, to, too, two, under, up, us, very, want, was, we, went, what, when, where, with, you*.

Exceptions to the "Rules"

Although much of the English language is phonically regular, there are many words that don't follow the above guidelines. For example, a particular combination of letters can represent more than one sound. Double *oo* can represent a long *oo* sound, as in words such as *boot, cool,* and *moon*; or it can represent a short *oo* sound, as in words such as *foot, good*, and *hook*. The letters *ow* can represent a diphthong, as in words such as *brow, fowl*, and *town*; or they can represent a long *o* sound, as in words such as *blow, snow,* and *tow*. Additionally, some high-frequency words such as *some, come, have,* and *said* do not follow the guidelines at all, and *ough* appears in such different-sounding words as *although, enough*, and *thought*.

The phonic guidelines provided in this book are just that—guidelines. They do not cover all the irregularities in our rich and varied language, but are intended to correspond roughly to the phonic lessons taught in the the first and second grades. Phonics provides the foundation for learning to read. Repetition, visual clues, context, and sheer experience provide the rest.